The ——
BIG
Crocodile
Book

The
BIG
Crocodile
Book

Acknowledgements: The editors and publishers wish to thank the following for giving permission to include in this anthology material which is their copyright. If we have inadvertently omitted to acknowledge anyone we should be most grateful if this could be brought to our attention for correction at the first opportunity. Andersen Press for *Crazy Charlie* by Ruth Brown. Edward Blishen for *Hare and Crocodile* by Edward Blishen. Random House Limited for *Don't Blame Me* and *Jungle School* by Richard Hughes from *The Wonder Dog*, published by Chatto & Windus. Eric Rolls for *Miss Strawberry's Purse* by Eric Rolls. Walker Books Limited for *Crocodile's Kin* by Colin McNaughton from *There's An Awful Lot of Weirdos In Our Neighbourhood* © 1987 Colin McNaughton. Published in the UK by Walker Books Limited.

A Red Fox Book

Published by Random House Children's Books
20 Vauxhall Bridge Road, London SW1V 2SA

A division of Random House UK Ltd.
London Melbourne Sydney Auckland
Johannesburg and agencies throughout the world

This compilation © Sally Grindley 1992
Text © the authors
Illustrations © the artists 1992

First published by Hutchinson Children's Books 1992

Red Fox edition 1994

Printed in China

RANDOM HOUSE UK Limited Reg. No. 954009

ISBN 0 09 925501 4

The

BIG

Crocodile
Book

Compiled by Sally Grindley

RED FOX

CONTENTS

WHAT DO CROCODILES
DRINK TEA OUT OF?

Crocory.

THE CROCODILE SNAPPY FACT FILE

Crocodiles are very special creatures. The next time you come across one in a book or face to face(!), you'll be looking at an animal whose ancestors were around a long, long time before ours. There were crocodiles already roaming the earth over 200 million years ago and their appearance has changed very little since then. They lived at the same time as the dinosaurs and managed to survive when the dinosaurs died out.

Close Relations

Like their ancient relatives, the dinosaurs, crocodiles are **reptiles.** This class of animals also includes turtles, tortoises, lizards and snakes. Reptiles hatch from eggs and most have scaly skin which they shed; they are all cold-blooded.

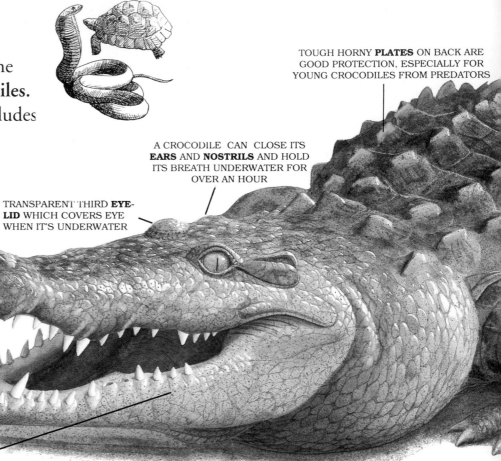

TOUGH HORNY **PLATES** ON BACK ARE GOOD PROTECTION, ESPECIALLY FOR YOUNG CROCODILES FROM PREDATORS

A CROCODILE CAN CLOSE ITS **EARS** AND **NOSTRILS** AND HOLD ITS BREATH UNDERWATER FOR OVER AN HOUR

TRANSPARENT THIRD **EYE-LID** WHICH COVERS EYE WHEN IT'S UNDERWATER

POWERFUL **JAWS** FOR CLAMPING PREY

How Hot Crocs Stay Cool

You can call a croc **cold-blooded,** but it won't mind, because this just means it cannot control its body temperature, which varies according to how hot or cold the croc's surroundings are. So during the day it will alternately bask in the sun and slide into cool water to stay the same temperature.

Where in the World are Crocodiles?

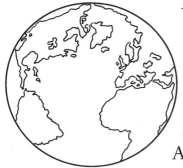

Most crocodiles live in freshwater rivers, lakes and swamps, though some, such as Australian salties, live in saltwater. They're found in tropical and subtropical parts of China, South-east Asia, South America and the Indian sub-continent, as well as North America, Australasia and Africa.

THE CROC USES ITS BIG POWERFUL **TAIL** TO DEFEND ITSELF, TO STUN PREY AND FOR SWIMMING

RESILIENT **SKIN** ALL OVER IS ALSO WATERTIGHT, SO A CROC NEVER SWEATS AND CAN'T DRY OUT

SHORT STRONG **LEGS** LIFT A CROC'S BELLY OFF THE GROUND WHEN IT WALKS. CROCS CAN RUN VERY FAST

QUIZ 1
In which of these places would you see crocodiles?
a) On a North Australian beach
b) Beneath the peaks of the Himalayas
c) On the coast of Greece
d) On the banks of the river Ganges
e) In a Norwegian fjord
ANSWER ON PAGE 92

Grub's Up

The crocodile eats all sorts of animals including fish, deer, wild pigs, antelopes, zebras and human beings. So watch out! It is a master of disguise when searching for prey. It

lies very still in the water, easily mistaken for a log, with only its eyes and nostrils visible. When it spots likely food it dashes out, clamps the animal between its jaws and drags it into the water, stunning it with its tail and drowning it. The croc may store the meat until it rots so it's easier to eat. Crocodiles are fierce, but not greedy - they share their food with each other.

QUIZ 2
How many meals does a crocodile eat a year?
a) 5
b) 50
c) 500
d) 5000
ANSWER ON PAGE 92

Crocodilians Galore

The crocodile is also a crocodilian. Its closest cousins

CAIMAN

← MAX. 4.6M →

ALLIGATOR

← MAX. 6M →

Crocodile Hall of Fame

The estuarine or saltwater crocodile from South-east Asia and Australia is the largest.

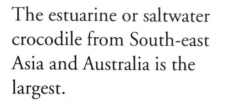

ADULT MALES
CAN WEIGH 500KG.

THAT'S AS MUCH AS EIGHT
FULLY - GROWN PEOPLE.

And if you think a stretch limousine is long ...

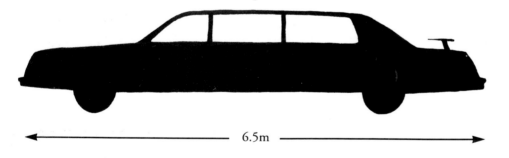

← 6.5m →

THE **OLDEST**
CROCODILES
CAN LIVE UP
TO 100 YEARS!

...the longest saltie can easily beat that!

← 9m →

It's seven and a half times as long as the smallest, Osborn's Dwarf crocodile from the Congo.

←1.2m→

are other crocodilians such as:

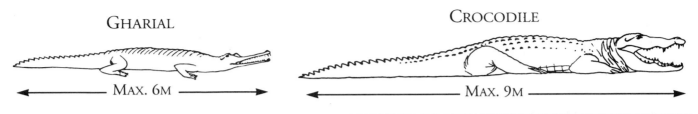

GHARIAL

CROCODILE

← —— MAX. 6M —— →

← —————— MAX. 9M —————— →

Crocodile Families

In the mating season a male crocodile chooses a female. He whirls around in the water and roars loudly before mating with her. The mother crocodile digs a pit or builds a nest of plants to lay her eggs in. She may lay up to 95 eggs at a time. She guards them without sitting on them- the sun and rotting vegetation will keep them warm until they hatch. Hatching babies make noises to tell their mother she should dig them out. She takes them to their nursery in the water, which they leave when they are big enough to be safe from predators.

QUIZ 3
Why does a mother crocodile put her babies in her mouth?
a) To keep them warm
b) To carry them to the nursery pool
c) Because she's feeling peckish.
ANSWER ON PAGE 92

When is a Crocodile an Alligator?

The easiest way to tell if that's really a crocodile smiling at you, is to look for the large fourth tooth on the bottom jaw. If you can see it when the mouth is closed it's a crocodile, if you can't then it's an alligator.

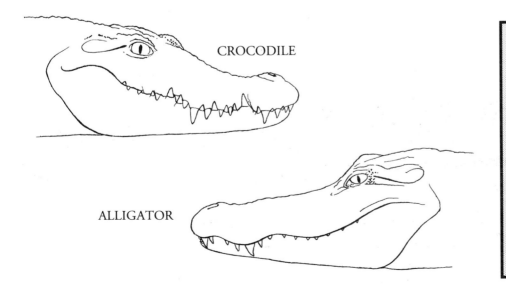

CROCODILE

ALLIGATOR

QUIZ 4
Can you guess which of these are real crocodiles?
a) Looter
b) New Guinea
c) Siamese
d) African Dwarf
e) Mugger
f) Halomista
g) Orinoco
h) Japanese
i) French Dancing
j) Tortoiseshell
ANSWER ON PAGE 92

Umbopa and the Crocodile

W.J. CORBETT

Little Umbopa's heart sank as he scrambled down the river bank. The bridge had been washed away by last night's storm. How was he supposed to cross the water and run all the errands he had to run that day?

The crocodile cruising around the remains of the bridge was full of sympathy. 'Bit of a nuisance, eh?' he said, cocking a cunning and popping eye.

'I'm due at my grandma's at eight o'clock sharp,' said Umbopa, worriedly. 'And grandma Twala always shouts at me when I'm late.'

'What you need is an emergency bridge,' said the crocodile, smoothly. 'A bridge like me, for instance. I'd be honoured to ferry little Umbopa across the river to his grandma Twala's house. For free, of course.'

'I've never heard of a free ferry-ride before,' said Umbopa, suspiciously. 'Especially not from a crocodile. What would you want in return?'

'Any return is the last thing on my mind,' grinned the crocodile, whose name was Gagool. 'So, come on, little Umbopa, hop aboard my back for the ride of your life. Unless you'd rather keep grandma Twala waiting and fuming. Don't tell me that a sturdy lad like you is afraid of his uncle Gagool?'

Umbopa was afraid. Everyone in his village feared the crafty crocodile, who was always cruising where the children were bathing. All the mothers in the village were wary about the health of their toes when they went down to the river to wash clothes and draw water. But Umbopa was desperate to cross to the other side. He feared his grandma's sharp tongue much more than he feared a whole riverful of cunning crocodiles. And he always had his 'motto' and training to call upon if Gagool's generous offer turned out to be false. So, confident that he could outwit Gagool in a crisis, he hopped aboard the crocodile's scaly back.

Halfway across the river Umbopa's worst fears came true.

'Now to do the dirty deed,' muttered Gagool to himself, as he writhed about in the water to savage his small passenger. But Umbopa was prepared.

'By the way, Gagool,' he said, trying to hide his terror as he cringed away from the crocodile's toothy snaps. 'Didn't I tell you that I'm going to grandma's to bring home my little sister? She's been spending the night there learning how to cook. If I don't deliver her safely home at nine o'clock sharp, my mother will shout at me even louder than grandma Twala does.'

'A double journey across the river of no return, eh? That's breakfast plus lunch in any crocodile language,' thought Gagool, smacking his tongue around his rows and rows of sharp teeth.

So he continued across the river, calling jovially over his scaly shoulder, 'And needless to say, little Umbopa, I

WHAT'S A CROCODILE'S
FAVOURITE CARD GAME?

Snap.

16

WHAT'S ITS SECOND
FAVOURITE CARD GAME?

Eat your neighbour.

demand the honour of ferrying you and your sister back home. For free, of course.'

'You're much too generous, Gagool,' cried Umbopa, leaping gratefully for the shore as they coasted in. 'I'll just run and pick up my little sister. You will wait?'

'Don't worry, I'll be waiting,' smiled Gagool, his mouth watering. He was picturing Umbopa's sister to be even plumper and sturdier than her brother.

'Sorry to keep you waiting, Gagool,' called Umbopa, slipping and sliding down the river bank, his fat little sister in tow. 'You'll be pleased to hear that grandma Twala didn't shout at me once. Thanks to you I was spot on time.'

'All good things are worth waiting for,' winked Gagool. 'Come on then, let's get you both safely home. We don't want mother shouting at us, eh?'

Umbopa's little sister was terrified as her brother ushered her aboard Gagool's scaly back. But Umbopa was confident that, with his motto and his training at the ready, he could outwit the crocodile if need be. Again, Gagool cruised to a stop in the middle of the river.

'Now to do two wickedly tasty, dirty deeds,' he muttered, his hungry jaws reaching over his shoulder to snap the children into pieces. But little Umbopa was quite prepared again.

'Oh, there's something I forgot to tell you, Gagool,' he said, hugging his weeping sister close. 'After I've delivered my sister home, me and my four friends want to cross back over the river. We've all won awards and we are going to be presented with them at exactly ten o'clock.'

'Five for the chop, eh? A tragedy that large will keep me in grub for days,' mused Gagool to himself, sucking his rows of sharp teeth. So he continued the journey, calling cunningly backwards, 'And I'll be very upset if I don't have the honour of ferrying little Umbopa and his friends back across the river. For free, of course.'

'Of course,' shouted Umbopa, grabbing his snivelling sister by the hand and leaping for the shore. 'Me and my friends won't be more than a few minutes, Gagool.'

'You've all got to get your football togs together, eh?' said Gagool, his belly rumbling and burping hungrily. 'Being awarded a prize for winning the five-a-side league, are you? Well, hurry back, for I'll be waiting impatiently. Uncle Gagool doesn't like being parted from his little Umbopa.'

For what seemed ages, he cruised around the remains of the bridge. Then, just when he thought that Umbopa and his football team weren't going to appear, they did, in full uniform. But it wasn't football strip they were wearing. Gagool realised that he had made a terrible mistake as he gazed pop-eyed at their kerchiefs and woggles, their bush hats and tightly clutched staffs. Ominously, every boy had a row of badges down his khaki sleeve. Gagool's heart sank as they solemnly filed aboard his scaly back.

Halfway across the river the crocodile's worst fears were realised. In a flash, Umbopa had slipped a noose around Gagool's jaws, binding them fast with a non-slip sailors' knot.

'Oh, me back . . . Oh, me tail . . . Oh, me poor ribs,' wheezed and groaned Gagool, as the Eagle Patrol of the Ethiopian Boy Scout Movement laid into him with their thwacking staffs. 'Have mercy on your old uncle Gagool . . .'

'That will teach you to terrorise the children and the ladies of our village,' said little Umbopa, as their battered ferry

wallowed gasping into shore. 'I never did tell you my motto, did I "uncle" Gagool? Well, it's BE PREPARED. And I hope for your sake that when we've been presented with our River Craft badges you'll be fully prepared to ferry us home again. For free, of course.'

'Of course,' snuffled the bruised Gagool through his swelling nose. 'Anything for my little Umbopa . . .'

And the chastened Gagool was as good as his word, since he had no choice. From that day on he became as good as gold, and came to enjoy his role as a ferry. A free one, of course.

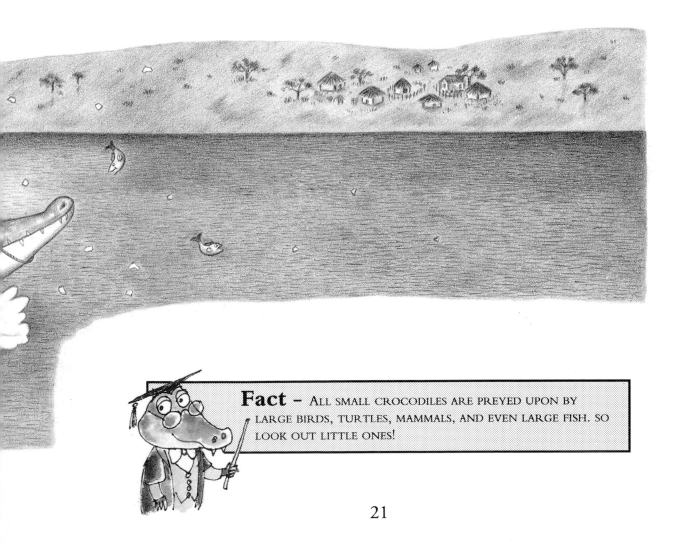

Fact – ALL SMALL CROCODILES ARE PREYED UPON BY LARGE BIRDS, TURTLES, MAMMALS, AND EVEN LARGE FISH. SO LOOK OUT LITTLE ONES!

Awful Love Song of the Crocodile

MIKE RATNETT

Come give me a kiss, my darling,
Give me a kiss my dear;
Whisper sweet nothings my angel,
Into my small green ear.
I know I'm a crinkly crocodile,
Squelching in the mud,
But the thought of one kiss,
From your sweet lips,
Heats my chilly blood.
Give me a kiss, my bunnykins,
Here, among the rushes;
A butterfly kiss on my long, green snout,
Reddened now with blushes.
Oh, give me a smacker, my lamb-chop,
Make my toes curl with delight!
Just one kissy-wissy my dumpling,
And I will try hard not to bite.

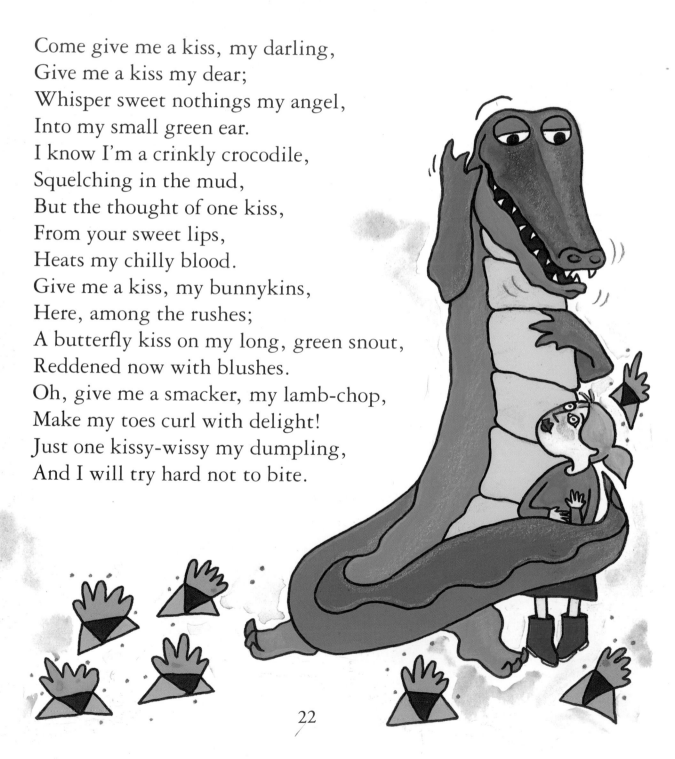

Don't Go to the Bathroom

MIKE RATNETT

'Please don't go to the bathroom, Father,
There's a crocodile having a soak;
He's there blowing bubbles and scrubbing his toes,
No, I promise this isn't a joke!'

'What nonsense, my boy!' answered Father,
'All crocs wash in rivers or rain.'
And he laughed all the way to the bathroom,
But we never saw Father again.

23

Crocodile's Teeth

ANON

A crocodile's teeth are a problem,
A crocodile's teeth are a pain;
A crocodile suffers from toothache
Again and again and again.

Now, getting the toothache so often
Makes crocodiles lose all their bite,
And desperate measures are called for
To bring back their lost appetite.

Thus crocodiles go to the dentist
On average, every eight years
(Quite by chance, that's precisely how often
A dentist somewhere disappears).

WHAT DO CROCODILES
DRINK AT PARTIES?

Crocktails.

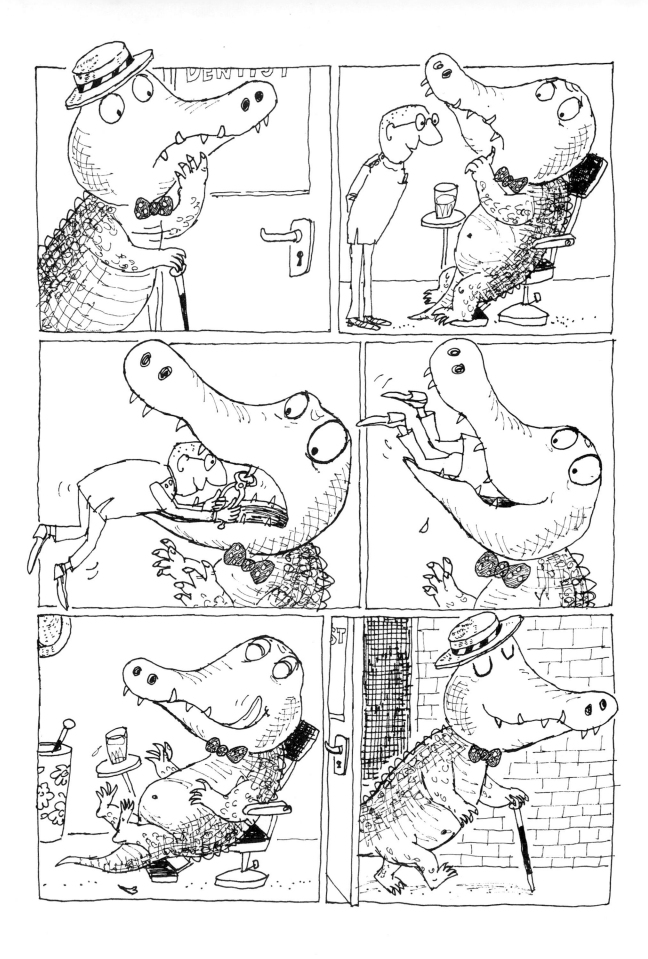

Crazy Charlie

RUTH BROWN

In the jungle, by the river, lived the biggest crocodile in the whole world. Crazy Charlie. That is what the other animals called him. He had the most enormous teeth and he ate everything he saw.

He started off in a small way, just munching the odd floating log or canoe. But then he got more ambitious and started to eat jetties and motor boats and bicycles. In fact anything or anyone anywhere near the river at any time was in danger of being crunched up by Charlie's mighty teeth.

People all over the world were shocked and horrified, but this only made Crazy Charlie worse, because the more famous he became the more he showed off.

He started eating houses and trains and factories. Things had gone too far!

The people called in the Army. The soldiers showered Charlie with arrows, to frighten him away, but he caught them and used them as toothpicks. They shot at him with a cannon but Charlie caught the cannonballs and crunched them up like gobstoppers.

They even fired a guided missile at him, but he ate that too – and enjoyed it. The people were in despair. But Crazy Charlie was having the time of his life being the centre of the world's attention.

But one day, something terrible happened to Charlie. One by one his huge, beautiful sharp teeth began to fall out.

Finally he was totally toothless. The crowds didn't come any more; nobody was frightened of him; nobody made a fuss. He was no longer big news. Life was very dull for Crazy Charlie. But the other animals enjoyed the peace and quiet.

One day, Charlie saw a tourist, the first he'd seen for about six months. The man, who was collecting plants, looked absolutely terrified when he stumbled over the crocodile dozing by the river. But Charlie knew that there was no point in trying to frighten the man. Who's afraid of a gummy crocodile anyway? So he just gave him a toothless grin instead. The man was so relieved that he smiled at Charlie.

'I know just what you need,' he said. 'I'll send you some when I get home.'

Charlie thought no more about him until a few months later, when a large parcel arrived for him. It was from the plant-collecting tourist. He was a dentist and he had made Charlie the most beautiful set of sparkling teeth!

WHAT DO YOU GET IF YOU CROSS A CROCODILE AND A LETTUCE?
A big green salad that eats you.

Crazy Charlie put them in his mouth and smiled the shiniest smile anyone had ever seen. People started flocking to see him once more, and how Charlie loved it! He was big news again, the centre of the world's attention, but now all he had to do was SMILE.

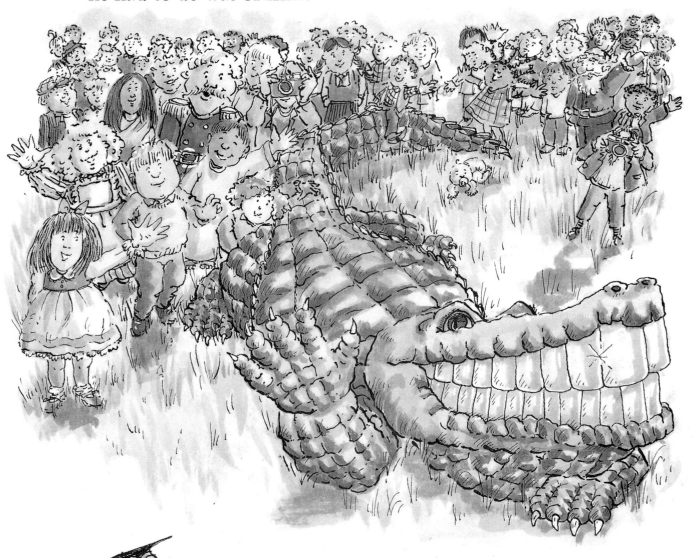

Fact – AFTER THEY'VE EATEN, CROCODILES SWALLOW STONES WHICH HELP THEM DIGEST THEIR FOOD. SOME VERY STRANGE THINGS HAVE BEEN FOUND INSIDE CROCODILES, INCLUDING BOTTLES, COINS, CARTRIDGE CASES, AND EVEN A THERMOS FLASK!

Don't Blame Me

RICHARD HUGHES

There was once a young man called Simon, who lived a long way from where he worked. So he thought, 'If I could only buy a nice motorbike to go to my work on, that would be fine.' So Simon saved up his money, till he thought he had nearly enough; and one Saturday he went off to the street where second-hand motorbikes were sold, to see if he could find one to suit him.

At almost the first shop he came to, there was a most grand-looking motorbike, almost new; and the price the man was asking seemed much too cheap for such a fine one. 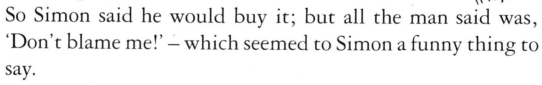 So Simon said he would buy it; but all the man said was, 'Don't blame me!' – which seemed to Simon a funny thing to say.

Simon bought it, and rode it home; and it went sweetly and well, and he was very pleased with it. So on Monday morning he started out on it to his work; and as he went he wondered what the man who sold it meant when he said, 'Don't blame me!'

Simon knew soon enough, though; for as he was riding

along a lonely piece of road, he felt the motorbike beginning to wriggle under him, as if it was coming to bits. It wasn't doing that, but it was doing something far worse – it was turning into a crocodile!

When Simon found he was riding a crocodile, he was more frightened than he had ever been before. He was too frightened to stay on its back; so he jumped off, and began to run for his life with the crocodile after him; and at first he left the crocodile a bit behind.

But presently Simon began to get so tired that the crocodile began to catch him up, and he thought he would have to give up and be eaten. Just then he saw a donkey in the road before him. He managed to run till he had caught up the donkey, and then he said:

'Mr Donkey, will you kindly give me a ride?'

But the donkey was a selfish one, not a nice donkey at all; and just because he saw Simon was really tired and needed a ride, he said, No, he wouldn't.

'You can jolly well walk,' he said. '*I* have to!'

'All right,' said Simon, 'then let me pass you,' for the road was rather narrow.

So the donkey let him pass; and Simon walked. Now that he had the donkey in between him and the crocodile, he didn't feel quite so frightened; so he didn't trouble to walk very fast.

Presently the donkey said:

'Hee-haw! Hee-haw! Simon, Simon, will you walk a little faster? There's a crocodile behind me, and he's snapped off my tail.'

But Simon wouldn't trouble to walk faster, and the donkey couldn't pass him to get away from the crocodile; so presently the donkey said:

'Hee-haw! Hee-haw! HEE-HAW! *Will* you walk a little faster, *please?* There's a crocodile behind me, and he's swallowed me all but my head.'

But even then Simon wouldn't trouble to walk any faster; and then at last he heard the donkey say in a faint, small voice:

'Hee-haw! Hee-haw! I'm *inside* the crocodile now!'

So then Simon knew he would have to run again, so away he went for his life, with the crocodile after him. But because he had had a good rest, at first he left the crocodile behind; and also, of course, the crocodile had a heavy donkey inside him now.

Presently in the road ahead of him Simon saw a giant.

'Mr Giant,' said Simon to the giant, 'will you kindly give me a ride?'

'Certainly!' said the giant kindly. 'Certainly, certainly, certainly!' So he picked up Simon and sat him on his shoulder, and went on strolling along the road, swing-ing his umbrella as he went. Presently Simon saw the crocodile

catching them up; but he didn't tell the giant, because he didn't quite know what to say.

'Ow!' the giant cried suddenly, and began to dance. 'I've been stung by a wasp!'

When the giant danced it was difficult for Simon to hold on; but somehow he managed, and looking down he saw what had really happened. It wasn't a wasp, it was the

33

crocodile who had bitten the giant, and who was holding on to the seat of the giant's trousers like grim death.

But the giant couldn't see that, because it was behind him and his neck was still. He just kept on dancing and swishing behind him with his umbrella. And though Simon was sorry to have got the kind giant into so much trouble, he wasn't going to let go. He just hung on and hoped for the best.

At last, by great good luck, the giant managed to hit the crocodile with his umbrella. Now, giants' umbrellas are generally magic, and this one certainly was. For no sooner did it touch the crocodile, than the crocodile turned back again into a motorbike, and just then Simon lost hold of the giant's collar and fell in the road with a frightful thump on his head.

The thump knocked him silly at first, but presently he sat up and opened his eyes. There was the motorbike lying in the road; a crowd of people was standing around.

'That's a nice motorbike you've got,' said one of them. 'Do you want to sell it?'

'Yes,' said Simon.

'Then I'll buy it,' said the other chap.

'All right,' said Simon, 'buy it if you like, but *Don't blame me!*'

For Simon saw then what none of the others saw. He saw the motorbike open its mouth and grin with all its wicked white teeth. And no wonder the motorbike was pleased! For the young man who had bought it was fat and juicy, and didn't look as if *he* could run an inch!

Cruel Miss Pring

IAN WHYBROW

'Cleo you're not listening!'
Shrilled the frightening Miss Pring.
'What did I just say to do
Once we get inside the Zoo?'

Cleo, though she tried to speak,
Found that she felt much too weak.
Trembling by the turnstile, she
Turned to her classmates twenty-three

And saw that they were innocent
Of what the wicked woman meant.
Where Cleo came from, by the Nile,
Teachers could not be so vile;

But cruel Miss Pring – yes – she had heard her –
Was planning hideous mass-murder!
For *this* is what she said to do
Once they had entered London Zoo:

'You will set off in single file,
Follow me quietly for a while,
And once we see the sign REPTILE,
Get into a crocodile!'

Hare and Crocodile

A TALE FROM UGANDA
RETOLD BY EDWARD BLISHEN

One day, Hare went to visit his sister. She'd married Crocodile, and they lived on an island in the middle of a lake, with all the other crocodiles. There were Aunt crocodiles, many of them, and Uncle crocodiles, many of the them, and crowds of Grandfather crocodiles, and Grandmother crocodiles. And there were crocodiles who were everybody else's nephews and nieces. Everywhere you looked there were crocodiles. Hare wouldn't have dreamed of going there if his sister hadn't married Crocodile. But she had, and so Hare felt perfectly safe.

And he was safe. They gave him a very good time. And all might have been well, except for one thing. Hare loved eating eggs. And one day he saw Crocodile putting his wife's eggs into the granary. That was where they kept the grain, and other things to eat. But in one corner of the granary, as Hare couldn't help noticing, Crocodile stored all those eggs. And Hare's mouth watered!

The next day Crocodile
and his wife went swimming,
and Hare stayed at home.
He said he had a headache
and just wanted to rest, quietly.

The moment they'd gone he hurried
to the granary and found the eggs.
They were big and yellow and
delicious. He ate as many as
he could and then collected
the shells and buried them.
He took care to wipe his mouth,
then waited for his sister and Crocodile.
Oh, he said when they arrived, he was very hungry. So his
sister cooked some food for him; but when it was brought,
Hare found he could eat nothing.
His stomach was full of egg.

He went to bed early, and by the morning he felt much
better. Again his sister and Crocodile went swimming.
Again Hare stayed at home, saying he needed to rest. And
again, I'm afraid, he went to the granary and feasted on those
delicious eggs.

In the end, there was only one egg left.

Hare thought he'd better bring his visit to an end. So that evening he said to Crocodile, 'I think I'll go home tomorrow. I've loved being here, but there are a number of things I must do at home. I'm sure you understand.' And Crocodile said yes, of course, and they'd loved having him.

In the morning they were about to leave, for Crocodile had to take Hare across the water on his back, when Crocodile said, 'I must just count the eggs before we go. I always count them at this time of year.'

'Oh, eggs!' said Hare. 'You have eggs, have you? I never knew you had eggs! Eggs, eh? Where do you keep them?' He felt dreadfully nervous.

'They're kept in the granary,' said Crocodile. 'Haven't you noticed them?'

'Noticed them?' said Hare. 'Goodness me, no! I had no idea! How many are there?'

'There are exactly seventy,' said Crocodile.

'I'd like to see them for myself,' said Hare.

'So you shall,' said Crocodile. 'In fact, if you like, you can count them for me.'

'Nothing would please me more,' said Hare. (And he meant it.) He climbed into the granary and then into the

WHAT'S FULL OF NUTS AND FRUIT AND DANGEROUS?

Crocodile Dundee cake

corner where the eggs were kept. 'Oh,' he cried. 'What wonderful eggs! Oh what fine big, yellow eggs! I say, I shall enjoy counting these!'

And he took the one remaining egg and lifted it up so Crocodile could see it. And Hare started counting. 'One,' he said, and lowered the egg to the bottom of the bin. Then he lifted the egg again, so Crocodile could see it, and said, 'Two.' He lowered it to the bottom of the bin, and lifted it again. 'Three.' And so he went on. '. . . Fifteen, sixteen . . .' he said. Sometimes he would stay down for a time, as if he was taking an egg from the far side of the bin. '. . . Thirty-one, thirty-two . . .' he said. And at last he came to: '. . . Sixty-nine, seventy!'

'Exactly seventy,' he called.

'Yes, I told you we had exactly seventy eggs,' said Crocodile. 'Well, that's done, then. They're all safe.' And after they'd said goodbye to Hare's sister, they set off for the lakeside. When they came to the water, Hare climbed on Crocodile's back, and Crocodile began swimming to the mainland, where Hare lived.

But not long after they'd gone, Crocodile's wife went into the granary to check for herself that the eggs were all there. She climbed into the bin. Horror! Only one egg left! She rushed at once to the edge of the lake. Half way across to the mainland she could see a splashing, and she knew that was Crocodile, swimming with Hare on his back. At the top of her voice she cried, 'Crocodile, Crocodile, Hare has eaten nearly all our eggs! He has eaten them all but one! Throw him in the lake! Drown him, drown him!'

'Is that my wife calling?' said Crocodile. 'It's so windy, I can't make out what she's saying.'

'I can hear her very well,' said Hare.

'What is she saying, then?'

'She's saying you could swim even faster if you wanted, because there's a strong wind behind us,' said Hare.

'Oh, good,' said Crocodile. 'Then I will swim faster, and you will get home sooner, my friend.'

And he did that, and Hare did get home sooner. They said goodbye, and Crocodile set off to swim home again.

But I have to tell you that Hare didn't think it wise to stay in his home a day longer. For some reason, he went to live far away, and when people asked him if his sister wasn't married to Crocodile, he'd pretend he was deaf, and hadn't heard what they said.

Crocodoll's Dream

CHRIS POWLING

Once, there was a Crocodoll.

He lived all alone on a glass display shelf high in the Dollmaker's window. On the next shelf down an Angeldoll lived next to a Robodoll. And on the shelf below that lived a lapful of Babydolls, so pretty you said coochy-coochy-coo the instant you saw them. 'We're gorgeous!' they exclaimed. 'We're really, really gorgeous! Can't you see how gorgeous we are?'

'And I'm tough as old boots,' said Robodoll.

'And I'm good as gold,' said Angeldoll.

But the Crocodoll said nothing.

Even now, after midnight, when dolls can do what they like because there's no one to keep them still by looking at them, the Crocodoll didn't say a word.

'What's up, Croc?' called the Babydolls. 'Are you in a sulk or something?'

'Maybe he's thinking,' Angeldoll said.

'Thinking?' said Robodoll. 'What's a Crocodoll got to think about?'

Angeldoll spread his wonderful wings and smiled. 'He's thinking he'd rather be an Angeldoll, good as gold, like me.'

'Or as tough as old boots like me,' said Robodoll.

'Or really, really gorgeous like us,' said the Babydolls.

'Anyone can see how gorgeous *we* are. But who'd want to hug a knobbly old Crocodoll? Look at his knobbly teeth and knobbly legs.'

'Look at his knobbly *body*,' said Robodoll.

'He's knobbly all over,' said Angeldoll with a shudder, 'from the top of his knobbly snout to the tip of his knobbly tail. No wonder he has to live up there on his own.'

'No wonder,' Robodoll nodded.

'No wonder,' echoed the Babydolls.

Still the Crocodoll stayed silent.

So none of them noticed the tear from his knobbly eye that ran down his knobbly face till it made a knobbly splash on the shop floor.

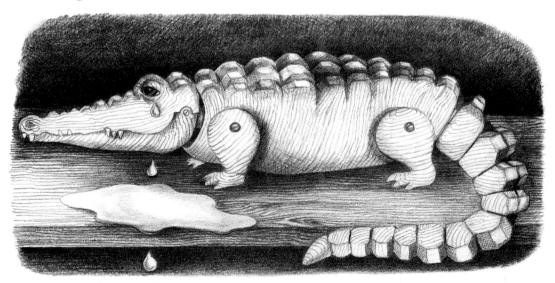

Suddenly, with a smart, soldierly salute, Robodoll stood to attention. 'Let's play our favourite game,' she suggested. 'Let's tell each other our dolldreams.'

'We'll start! We'll start!' cried the Babydolls.

The dream of the Babydolls was cuddles and nappy-changes all day long – maybe after dark, too, if there was a nightlight. 'Won't it be *lovely?*' they squeaked.

Robodoll's dream was nonstop battles, starting before dawn and finishing beyond dusk, with or without a nightlight. 'Won't it be splendid?' she breathed.

In his dream, Angeldoll looked down from a Christmas tree at a roomful of family, opening presents. 'Only once a year,' he told them. 'But year after year it'll go on – by candlelight, not nightlight. Won't it be heavenly?'

'Heavenly,' agreed Robodoll and the Babydolls.

But each meant their *own* dream, of course. Lying back on their shelves in the moonshiny window, they dreamed and dreamed their dolldreams . . . till they heard a small, knobbly cough.

A *knobbly* cough?

From high on the top shelf, a knobbly voice not much louder than a hiccup said, 'I've got a dream, too.'

'You?' said Angeldoll.

'What can a Crocodoll dream?' sniffed Robodoll.

'A knobbly dream,' giggled the Babydolls. 'A knobbly Crocodream . . . that's what a Crocodoll dreams.'

'Is it?' Angeldoll asked. 'Tell us, Crocodoll.'

The Crocodoll sighed. 'You'll only laugh if I do.'

'No we won't,' said Robodoll. 'We promise.'

'We promise,' the Babydolls said.

So the Crocodoll told them everything. His words were as soft and as shy as the tick of a knobbly clock that's about to stop altogether. 'Mostly it's brightness,' he said. 'A starshiny brightness that lights up every knobble I've got – on my teeth, on my legs, on my body – from the top of my knobbly snout to the tip of my knobbly tail. Only it doesn't matter, you see. People *like* my knobbliness. They whistle and stamp and cheer at me . . . in my dream.'

'Starshiny brightness?' said Angeldoll.

'Whistling and stamping and cheering?' said Robodoll.

'Because they *like* your knobbliness?' said the Babydolls. 'Who could possibly like knobbliness?'

And they burst out laughing so loudly and for such a long time, the Dollmaker came yawning and grumbling downstairs to keep them still with a look.

After this, the Crocodoll never spoke again.

Not even when Angeldoll and Robodoll and everyone of the Babydolls left the shop with their new owners. Not even when the Dollmaker filled her shelves with more dolls – a Discodoll, a Clowndoll and an Aliendoll along with some Babydolls eager for coochy-coochy-coos.

Not even when these were sold, too.

Alone on his top shelf, the Crocodoll watched the comings and goings below and stayed as cheerful as he could. 'No more tears for me,' he told himself. 'I mean, it's not my fault I'm knobbly. And it's not the Dollmaker's fault my dream is an impossible dream.'

So he was quite surprised on the day the Dollmaker reached up for him. 'Your turn at last,' she said. 'I'm sorry it's been so long – life's really hectic these days. It's about time I finished you off . . .'

Finished him off?

The Crocodoll held his breath as the Dollmaker carried him to her bench.

Soon she was hard at work.

First came rings – tiny rings – in his body and legs, in his snout and his tail. Then came strings – wiry strings – but so thin he could barely feel their weight as the Dollmaker tied them in place. Last of all came varnish – quick-drying varnish – on a brush that tickled him everywhere, inch by knobbly inch.

'You'll look so *shiny* under the spotlights,' she told him.

'Spotlights?' thought the Crocodoll.

'And so you should,' the Dollmaker went on. 'Why, along with Wendy and Captain Hook and Peter himself, you're one of the stars of the show.'

'A star of the show?' the Crocodoll blinked.

The Dollmaker stepped back to check her handiwork. 'It strikes me you're a thoroughly handsome Crocopuppet!' she smiled.

A Croco*puppet*?

As the Dollmaker tucked him under her arm and hurried across the town square to the puppet theatre opposite, he saw a queue at the box office already – mums and dads and hoppity kids all keen to book tickets for the show.

PETER PAN – said the posters outside – COMING SOON.

Of course, he realised it wouldn't be easy. He'd need hours and hours of practice. He'd have to be tougher than old boots, at least as good as gold and much, much more gorgeous than a coochy-coochy-coo . . . for when the curtain swished up, the lights flooded down and everyone there began to whistle and stamp and cheer, then – for the first time ever – he could move as much as he liked *even though there were people looking at him!* 'After all, I'm not a *doll*, am I?' he whispered.

And the Crocopuppet beamed with happiness.

The King of the Crocodiles
A TRADITIONAL TALE
FROM THE PUNJAB

Once upon a time a farmer went out to look at his fields by the side of the river, and found to his dismay that all his young green wheat had been trodden down, and nearly destroyed, by a number of crocodiles, which were lying lazily amid the crops like great logs of wood. He flew into a great rage, bidding them go back to the water, but they only laughed at him.

Every day the same thing occurred – every day the farmer found the crocodiles lying in his young wheat, until one morning he completely lost his temper, and, when they refused to budge, began throwing stones at them. At this they rushed on him fiercely, and he, quaking with fear, fell on his knees, begging them not to hurt him.

'We will hurt neither you nor your young wheat,' said the biggest crocodile, 'if you will give us your daughter in marriage; but if not, we will eat you for throwing stones at us.'

The farmer, thinking of nothing but saving his own life, promised what the crocodiles required of him; but when, on his return home, he told his wife what he had done, she was very much vexed, for their daughter was as beautiful as the moon, and her betrothal into a very rich family had already taken place. So his wife persuaded the farmer to disregard the promise made to the crocodiles, and proceed with his daugh-

ter's marriage as if nothing had happened; but when the
wedding day drew near the bridegroom died, and there was
an end to that business. The farmer's daughter, however, was
so beautiful that she was very soon asked in marriage again,
but this time her suitor fell sick of a lingering illness; in
short, so many misfortunes occurred to all concerned that at
last even the farmer's wife acknowledged the crocodiles must
have something to do with the bad luck. By her advice the
farmer went down to the river bank to try to induce the

crocodiles to release him from his promise, but they would hear of no excuse, threatening fearful punishments if the agreement were not fulfilled at once.

So the farmer returned home to his wife very sorrowful; she, however, was determined to resist to the uttermost, and refused to give up her daughter.

The very next day the poor girl fell down and broke her leg. Then the mother said, 'These demons of crocodiles will certainly kill us all! Better to marry our daughter to a strange house than see her die.'

Accordingly, the farmer went down to the river and informed the crocodiles they might send the bridal procession to fetch the bride as soon as they chose.

The next day a number of female crocodiles came to the bride's house with trays full of beautiful clothes, and henna for staining the bride's hands. They behaved with the utmost politeness, and carried out all the proper ceremonies with the greatest precision. Nevertheless the beautiful bride wept, saying, 'Oh, mother! Are you marrying me into the river? I shall be drowned!'

In due course the bridal procession arrived, and all the village was wonderstruck at the magnificence of the arrangements. Never was there such a retinue of crocodiles, some playing instruments of music, others bearing trays upon trays full of sweetmeats, garments and jewels, and all dressed in the richest of stuffs. In the middle, a perfect blaze of gold and gems, sat the King of the Crocodiles.

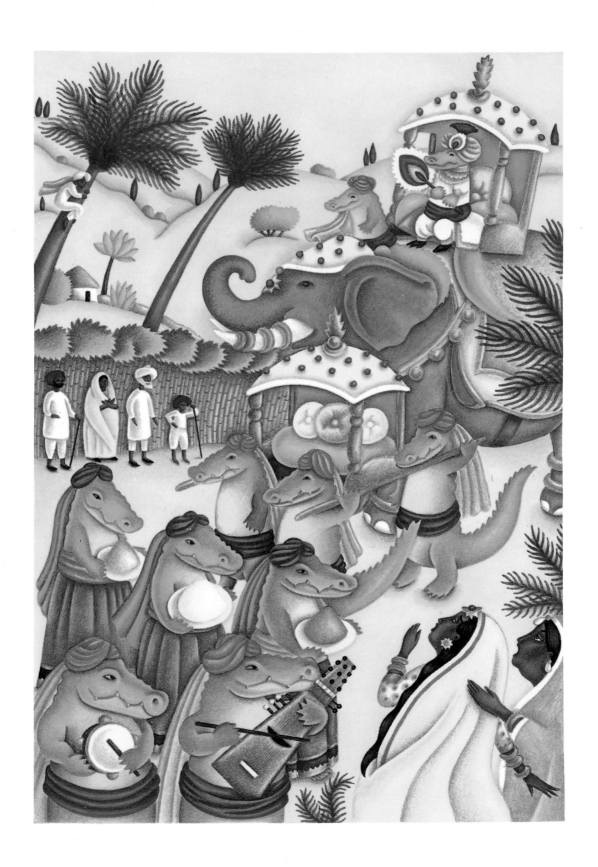

The sight of so much magnificence somewhat comforted the beautiful bride; nevertheless she wept bitterly when she was put into the gorgeous bride's palanquin and borne off to the river bank. Arrived at the edge of the stream, the crocodiles dragged the poor girl out, and forced her into the water, despite her struggles, for, thinking she was going to be drowned, she screamed with terror; but lo and behold! no sooner had her feet touched the water than it divided before her, and, rising up on either side, showed a path leading to the bottom of the river, down which the bridal party disappeared, leaving the bride's father, who had accompanied her so far, upon the bank, very much astonished at the marvellous sight.

Some months passed by without further news of the crocodiles. The farmer's wife wept because she had lost her daughter, declaring that the girl was really drowned, and her husband's fine story about the stream dividing was a mere invention.

Now when the King of the Crocodiles was on the point of leaving with his bride, he had given a piece of brick to her father, with these words: 'If ever you want to see your daughter, go down to the river, throw this brick as far as you can into the stream, and you will see what you will see!'

Remembering this, the farmer said to his wife, 'Since you are so distressed, I will go myself and see if my daughter be alive or dead.'
Then he went to the river bank, taking the brick, and

threw it ever so far into the stream. Immediately the waters rolled back from before his feet, leaving a dry path to the bottom of the river. It looked so inviting, spread with clean sand and bordered by flowers, that the farmer hastened along it without the least hesitation, until he came to a magnificent palace, with a golden roof, and shining, glittering diamond walls. Lofty trees and gay gardens surrounded it, and a sentry paced up and down before the gateway.

'Whose palace is this?' asked the farmer of the sentry, who replied that it belonged to the King of the Crocodiles.

'My daughter at least has a splendid house to live in!' thought the farmer; 'I only wish her husband were half as handsome!'

Then, turning to the sentry, he asked if his daughter were within.

'Your daughter!' returned the sentry, 'What should she do here?'

'She married the King of the Crocodiles, and I want to see her.'

At this the sentry burst out laughing. 'A likely story, indeed!' he cried. 'What! MY master married to YOUR daughter! Ha! Ha! Ha!'

Now the farmer's daughter was sitting beside an open window in the palace, waiting for her husband to return from hunting. She was as happy as the day was long, for you must know that in his own river-kingdom the King of the Crocodiles was the handsomest young Prince anybody ever set eyes upon; it was only when he went on shore that he assumed the form of a crocodile. So what with her magnifi-

cent palace and splendid young Prince, the farmer's daughter had been too happy even to think of her old home; but now, hearing a strange voice speaking to the sentry, her memory awakened, and she recognised her father's tones. Looking out she saw him there, standing in his poor clothes, in the glittering court; she longed to run and fling her arms round his neck, but dared not disobey her husband, who had forbidden her to go out of, or let anyone into the palace without his permission. So all she could do was to lean out of the window, and call to him, saying, 'Oh, dearest father! I am here! Only wait till my husband, the King of the Crocodiles returns, and I will ask him to let you in. I dare not without his leave.'

The father, though overjoyed to find his daughter alive, did not wonder she was afraid of her terrible husband, so he waited patiently.

In a short time a troop of horsemen entered the court. Every man was dressed from head to foot in armour made of glittering silver plates, but in the centre of all rode a Prince clad in gold – bright burnished gold, from the crown of his head to the soles of his feet – the handsomest, most gallant young Prince that ever was seen.

Then the poor farmer fell at the gold-clad horseman's feet, and cried, 'O King, cherish me! For I am a poor man whose daughter was carried off by the dreadful King of the Crocodiles!'

Then the gold-clad horseman smiled, saying, 'I am the King of the Crocodiles! Your daughter is a good, obedient wife, and will be very glad to see you.'

After this there were great rejoicings and merry-makings, but when a few days had passed away in feasting, the farmer became restless, and begged to be allowed to take his daughter home with him for a short visit, in order to convince his wife the girl was well and happy. But the Crocodile King refused, saying, 'Not so! But if you like I will give you a house and land here; then you can dwell with us.'

The farmer said he must first ask his wife, and returned home, taking several bricks with him to throw into the river and make the stream divide.

His wife would not at first agree to live in the Crocodile Kingdom, but she consented to go there on a visit, and afterwards became so fond of the beautiful river country that she was constantly going to see her daughter the Queen; till at length the old couple never returned to shore, but lived all together in the Crocodile Kingdom with their son-in-law, the King of the Crocodiles.

How Doth the Little Crocodile

LEWIS CARROLL

How doth the little crocodile
  Improve his shining tail,
And pour the waters of the Nile
  On every golden scale!

How cheerfully he seems to grin,
  How neatly spreads his claws,
And welcomes little fishes in
  With gently smiling jaws!

The Crocodile's Brushing his Teeth

COLIN McNAUGHTON

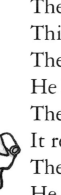

The crocodile's brushing his teeth, I'm afraid,
This certainly means we're too late.
The crocodile's brushing his teeth, I'm afraid,
He has definitely put on some weight.
The crocodile's brushing his teeth, I'm afraid,
It really is, oh, such a bore.
The crocodile's brushing his teeth, I'm afraid,
He appears to have eaten class four!

If You Should Meet a Crocodile

ANON

If you should meet a crocodile,
Don't take a stick and poke him;
Ignore the welcome in his smile,
Be careful not to stroke him.
For as he sleeps upon the Nile,
He thinner gets and thinner;
But whene'er you meet a crocodile
He's ready for his dinner.

61

There's a Crocodile in the Pond

DAVID COX

'No there isn't,' said the others.
    'There is, a great big crocodile.'
    'How big?'
    'As big as this.'

Daniel stretched out his arms as wide as he could.
    'He is not that big.'
    'He might even be bigger.'
    A pair of eyes watched them from the pond.
    'The crocodile has got big sharp teeth!'
    'Can he get out?'
    'Sometimes.'
    'Like when?'
    'Like when he's hungry and somebody's near enough to
bite.' They all took a step backwards.

'How come I've never seen him then?' said the boy with the freckles.

'Because he's a crafty crocodile, he's very good at hiding. You never know where he might be.'

'Where is he now?' said the boy, stepping nearer the water's edge.

The eyes in the water slowly moved.

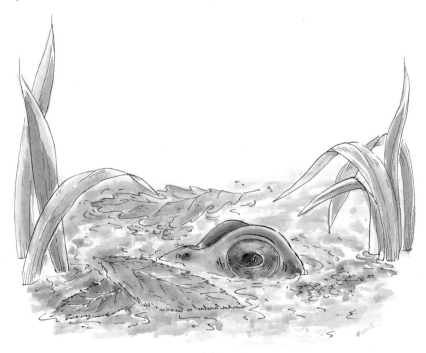

'You see all those leaves floating by the ducks?'
'Yeah!'
'He's right underneath them!'
'What's he doing under there?'
'He's making up his mind.'
'Making up his mind about what?'
'Whether to eat one of the ducks . . .'
'Or . . .'
'Or what??'
'Or jump out and eat one of you!'
'Eeeekk!' squealed the girl with the red ribbon.

'Why doesn't he eat *you* then?'

'Because I know him!'

'No you don't.'

'Yes I do – shall I call him out to eat you?'

'No, let him eat one of the ducks!'

The pair of eyes sticking up out of the water moved closer and closer. Suddenly ... the ducks took flight, a loose feather floated down to the water.

'Look! He nearly got one of the ducks!' screamed the girl.

'You know what that means, don't you?' said Daniel.

'That ducks are quicker than crocodiles?' said the blond haired boy.

'Yes, and that boys and girls are slower. He'll have to eat one of you now.' The yellow eyes blinked in the murky water just a few feet away from the edge.

'I'm going to get him out here,' said Daniel. He ran behind a tree just by the edge of the pond.

'Don't call the crocodile, he'll eat us all!'

The yellow eyes blinked once again.

'Rrrrrrrraaaaaahhhhhh!'

The children screamed and squealed as from behind the tree on all fours, frowning and snapping his jaws emerged . . . Daniel!

'RRRrrrrr . . . . I am the crocodile and I'm hungry, which one of you shall I eat first?'

The children ran half terrified, half laughing in all directions as Daniel the crocodile chased them.

The pair of eyes in the water suddenly hopped up onto a piece of wood.

'Rib-bit,' croaked the frog as he watched Daniel snapping and roaring around the park.

'So that's what a crocodile looks like,' thought the frog. And then he hopped back into the pond . . .

Miss Strawberry's Purse

ERIC C. ROLLS

Miss Strawberry has a long fat purse
To keep her money in.
It is a rare and handsome purse
Made of crocodile skin.
It is crocodile skin without a doubt
For she did not take the crocodile out
And when she walks to town to shop
He follows behind her clop, clop-clop,
And opens his mouth and bellows aloud
And swishes his tail amongst the crowd.
Now and again there's an angry mutter
As a man is swept into the gutter.

When in a shop it is time to pay
Shopkeepers look at the brute in dismay
When Miss Strawberry says, 'Crocky, open wide,'
And, 'Shopman, your money is deep inside.
Just dodge the slashing of his paws
And reach beyond those ugly jaws;
But I warn you if you make him cough
He'll probably bite your arm right off.'
The shopkeeper usually says, 'No worry.
Pay next month. I'm in no hurry.'
But a grocer once, owed four pounds ten,
Said, 'That's worth more than one of my men.'
He called his errand boy, 'Hey son,
Come over here, we'll have some fun.
I'll hold your legs and guard you while

You crawl in this quiet old crocodile
And collect in his vitals four pounds ten.
If you bring it out again
I'll give you sixpence for your trouble.
Come here, son, and at the double!'
Now the length of Miss Strawberry's crocodile's throat
Is four times as long as a shopkeeper's coat.
The crocodile opened fearfully wide
And the errand boy crawled right down inside.
When he had gathered four pounds ten
And hurriedly tried to back out again,
The crocodile closed his jaws with a smile,
Saying, 'One of the joys of a crocodile,
Indeed you might say, his favourite joy,
Is making a meal of a messenger boy.'

The Jungle School

RICHARD HUGHES

One day all the animals in the jungle met together and decided to have a school for their cubs. It was the parrot's idea:

'You see how clever and big going to school makes men and women grow,' she said; 'perhaps it would do the same for us.'

So they all made up their minds to have a school; and next they had to decide who was to be mistress.

'I will be mistress,' said the elephant's daughter, 'because I can smack them with my long trunk.'

But when the other animals thought of their poor little cubs being smacked by so enormous a mistress, they thought, No, she won't do.

'I will be mistress,' said the monkey, 'because I'm so clever at stealing, and I will teach them all to steal as well as me.'

At that all the other animals were terribly shocked and angry, and chased the monkey away as far as they could.

'*I* will be mistress,' said the crocodile's daughter.

'Why?' said the other animals.

'Because I have nothing better to do,' said the crocodile, and shut her jaws with a snap.

So that was settled; and the next thing to decide was, *where* the school was to be. Some wanted it in one place, and some in another; it all depended on where they lived themselves.

'Let's have it up a tree,' suddenly piped up the monkey, who had crept back again.

At that they were all angry with the poor little monkey again, and roared and hissed and bellowed at her so hard that once again she ran away in fright.

'We will have the school in the middle of my swamp!' said Miss Crocodile, and again she shut her jaws with a snap.

None of the others liked the idea; but they hadn't been able to agree on any other place amongst themselves, and since she was to be mistress, they thought it really was for her to decide.

When the morning came, all the big animals brought their cubs down to the edge of the swamp. There they had to leave them, for the swamp was too quaky for the big, heavy animals to walk on: it was bad enough for the cubs, who were lighter. And even then they floundered and splashed about in the oozy mud, and actually had to swim in places; and some of them, especially the ones who hated getting wet, were rather frightened. But they were brave little cubs, and

at last they all got to the crocodile's own pool right in the middle. Miss Crocodile had an old cracked bell in her wrinkled claw, and she was ringing it as hard as she could.

So all that morning she taught them lessons. But all she taught them was things about the swamp: muddy and oozy things, about rushes, and swamp-plants, and the sorts of slippery and creepy things that live in the swamp,  and how to tell one kind of smelly slime from another.

Then dinner-time came, so the cubs all said: 'Please, Miss, may we go home now for our dinners?'

'No, my dears,' said Miss Crocodile, grinning with all her teeth, 'you will all stay here, for *my* dinner!' And with that she seized the poor little bear-cub, who was the fattest and most roly-poly of all, and gobbled him up!

When all the father and mother animals found their cubs didn't come home for dinner, they were worried; so they came down to the edge of the swamp and shouted. But Miss Crocodile didn't even bother to answer. So all the cubs called out together: 'We can't come back; she's eating us! She says she will eat us all up, one by one!'

At that the animals were terribly upset; but there was nothing they could do, because none of them was light enough to walk on the quaky swamp. They howled and they bellowed and they roared; but they couldn't go into the swamp to save their cubs. And they could roar their heads off, for all Miss Crocodile minded. But as for that little monkey, she didn't say anything. She knew it was one thing the animals weren't clever enough to manage on their own; so she hurried straight away through the trees to where there was a ruined palace hidden in the jungle, to see if there was anyone left in it who would give her advice.

When she got there the palace was all tumbled down and overgrown with creepers and trees; even more than she remembered it. At first she thought it was quite empty and dark; but she went on exploring, and at last she found one room where there was still an old man sitting. He was spinning cobwebs as cleverly as any spider.

So the monkey told him what was the trouble and asked him what to do.

'First you must learn to spin cobwebs,' said the old man.

So he gave her a jar of the shiny, gluey stuff he used for spinning them from, and taught her how to do it.

'Now,' he said, 'you must spin a rope of this stuff, strong enough for you to swing on, and tie it to a tree, and then you'll be able to swing it right out over the middle of the swamp.'

'But if I do that,' said the monkey, 'the crocodile will just snap with her jaws and gobble me.'

'You must sit in this magic basket,' said the old man; 'then she won't be able to see you, and you must give her this bowl of soup.'

'Is it poison?' asked the monkey.

'No,' said the old man, 'it is the very best soup. But listen.

You must also give her this spoon to eat it with.'

'What then?' said the monkey.

'That's all,' said the old man. 'Go and do as I tell you.'

So the monkey took the jar of stuff for making cobwebs, and the magic basket, and the bowl of soup, and the spoon, and went back to the edge of the swamp. There she spun a rope strong enough to swing on, and tied it to a tree. Then she swung out on it, right over the middle of the swamp.

Miss Crocodile opened her jaws wide to snap up the little monkey; but the monkey just slipped into the magic basket in time.

'Where are you?' said the crocodile crossly. 'I can't see you.'

'I've brought you this bowl of soup,' said the monkey.

'Is it poison?' asked the crocodile.

'No, on my honour it is the best soup.'

When the monkey said that, the crocodile knew it must be true, for the animals never tell lies, even to their worst enemies, when they say something 'on their honour'.

'And here is a spoon to eat it with,' said the monkey; and gave the crocodile the spoon.

So the crocodile took the spoon and began to eat the soup.

Now the soup was the most lovely soup she had ever tasted, and quite safe; but the spoon was a magic one. At first the crocodile ate her soup in a genteel sort of way, just tipping it out of the spoon into her mouth. If she had kept on like that she would have been all right; but the soup was *so* good she soon got greedy, and started putting the spoon right inside her mouth.

Now the spoon, as I told you, was a magic spoon, and as soon as she put it in her mouth the magic began. The spoon began to swell; it stuck between her teeth, and she couldn't get it out of her mouth again. Still it went on swelling, till it fixed her jaws wide open, and still she couldn't get it out.

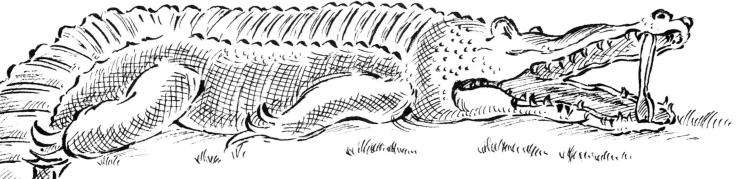

Then the monkey started spinning cobwebs; and in about ten minutes she had spun the wicked crocodile up so tight in cobwebs she couldn't move; she couldn't even wiggle her tail.

'Quick!' called the monkey to the cubs. 'Come on!'

So one by one the cubs climbed into the basket; and because it was a magic basket, as each cub climbed in the basket got bigger, so at last there was room for them all. They were just going to escape, when suddenly they heard a little voice say, 'Wait for me' – and there was the little bear-cub, just wriggling out of Miss Crocodile's open jaws! So then the monkey swung them all back safe and sound to dry land.

Then the animals were all so glad, and were sorry they had been so horrid to the little monkey before, and wanted to make it up to her.

'I tell you what,' they said, 'now you shall be schoolmistress instead, and you shall teach them whatever you like.'

'No,' said the monkey, 'I don't think I should really be a good schoolmistress, after all. But why not take them to the wise old man who lives in the ruined palace, and ask him to be their teacher?'

So that is what the animals, very sensibly, did; and the old man said he would do it, and made a school for them in the ruins and taught them all kinds of things, many of which were magic. So all the cubs grew up wise and clever; so wise and clever that they were soon much wiser and cleverer than any of the ordinary men and women who lived in that country; much too wise and clever, by the time they were grown up, ever to let a crocodile be schoolmistress to *their* children.

Fact – HAVE YOU HEARD THE EXPRESSION 'CROCODILE TEARS' USED WHEN PEOPLE PRETEND TO BE UPSET BUT DON'T REALLY MEAN IT? CROCODILES CRY NOT BECAUSE THEY ARE UNHAPPY, BUT BECAUSE IT'S HOW THEY GET RID OF A LOT OF SALT FROM THEIR BODIES.

Uncle's Old Croc

COLIN WEST

'Come for a ride!' my uncle said,
'I've got a great Old Croc.
The seats are made of leather, though
They're all as hard as rock.

'But it can get up quite a speed,
Especially downhill.
And when it goes round roundabouts,
It makes me feel quite ill.'

And so I went with Uncle, but
I came in for a shock:
For by the parking meter, there
Was standing his 'Old Croc'.

It had four feet instead of wheels
And snout instead of bonnet.
You should have seen the people stare
When we both rode upon it!

The Quiet Place

ANGELA McALLISTER

The animals were arguing among themselves about who was the greatest.

'I am the king of the beasts,' said lion. 'My roars echo through the mountains. There is no one as fierce as me.'

'You may be fierce,' said zebra, 'but look at my stripes. I am the most beautiful.'

Gazelle laughed. 'Who cares about being fierce or beautiful?' she said. 'I can run as fast as the wind.' And so they disagreed.

Above their heads a little bird hopped onto a branch.

'Poor little plover,' said lion. 'She isn't fierce, or beautiful or fast.'

But before plover could speak up for herself, a large crocodile crawled towards them. When the other animals saw crocodile they twitched nervously.

One by one crocodile looked at them all. 'Can anyone help me?' she asked, with a smile that showed a hundred sharp teeth. 'I am looking for a very quiet place, somewhere quite out of the way.'

Now, lion knew a quiet spot where he liked to lay in the sun, but he was too afraid to take crocodile there. Zebra knew a quiet place where she went to admire herself in the water, but she was too afraid to go off with crocodile. And gazelle knew a quiet place where she like to watch the sun go down, but she was too afraid to walk alone with crocodile.

'No,' they all said quickly. 'We're very sorry but we can't help you.'

Crocodile sighed and rubbed her long belly. 'I really must find somewhere soon,' she said.

Then plover hopped down from the trees above. 'I can help you,' she said. 'I know a quiet shady place by the river, where the mud is cool. Just follow me.'

The other animals watched them go with heavy hearts.

'That little bird is braver than all of us,' said lion, the king of the beasts.

'We should be ashamed of ourselves for being so afraid,' said zebra, as crocodile and bird disappeared.

'Let's go after them,' said gazelle, 'to see that plover comes to no harm.'

So the animals followed the path down to the river bank, and, hiding behind a tree, were amazed by what they saw. For there was crocodile digging a shallow pit – with the little bird sitting on her back!

'Foolish plover,' thought zebra, and was about to shout a warning to her, when she heard the crocodile speak:

'You were the only one who wasn't afraid to help me,' she said sadly, shedding a tiny crocodile tear.

Plover laughed, as she hopped off her back. 'The others may be fierce and beautiful and fast,' she said, 'but they are not always wise. They thought you were looking for a quiet spot to enjoy a meal, and that the meal might be them! But I knew why you rubbed your long belly, crocodile . . .'

Crocodile settled into the shallow pit and began to lay her eggs. In time her babies would hatch from them and she would carry them down to the nursery pool at the water's edge.

And the lion, the zebra and the gazelle, seeing how foolish they had been, slipped quietly away. No one felt like arguing about who was the greatest any more. Instead they all agreed on one thing – the little plover was the wisest of them all.

Fact – CROCS HAVE THEIR VERY OWN TEETH-CLEANING SERVICE! WHEN A CROCODILE IS LYING WITH ITS MOUTH OPEN TO COOL DOWN, A PLOVER WILL OFTEN LAND ON ITS JAW AND PICK AT THE FOOD CAUGHT BETWEEN THE CROCODILE'S TEETH.

from INVERSNAID, Gerard Manley Hopkins

... What would the world be, once bereft
Of wet and wildness? Let them be left,
O let them be left, wildness and wet;
Long live the weeds and the wilderness yet.

The Song of Crocodile

JUDY HINDLEY

Crocodile was dying. The Witch of Waters came and sat beside him. It was a strange sight. The Witch of Waters is a soft thing — a trembling, shivering creature, just like water. But, like water, she slips between your fingers if you try to catch her. And, like water, she can get round anything. So she was not afraid of Crocodile. In fact, she was fond of him, though you might not have guessed it.

She said to him, 'Well, old monster, it seems your time on Earth is finished. The hunters are after you. They've found your secret places. They've killed nearly all your tribe. Soon, you will be the last one left, and they will get you, too.'

As she spoke, Crocodile lunged at her angrily with his great, snapping jaws, but she dissolved into a cloud of sparkling droplets, and reappeared on the other side of him, out of reach.

'Poor Crocodile,' she sang, in a rather jeering, silvery voice. 'Of course, you've been a hunter, too. The oceans of fish that you and your lot have swallowed! And those poor frogs! Birds' eggs, too, I believe, and all sorts of little creatures that try to scratch their livings from the water's edge. And even people, now and then.'

'Not people,' said Crocodile sulkily. 'Well . . . not many. Don't like the taste, much. Our cousins, the Estuarines, have a fancy for human beings, but they're an odd bunch.'

'Still,' said the Witch, 'you knew you could do it if you had to. Those huge, powerful jaws of yours, that slashing tail! The way you would drag them underwater, until they drowned . . . poor, weak, two-legged creatures! Overgrown frogs, that's what you used to call them . . .'

'Ummmm,' said Crocodile, rather uneasily.

'And now, they've got you on the run,' the Witch continued. 'They've got you cornered. Soon, there'll be nothing left of you but belts and handbags and shoes. And they'll get tired of those, too. And that's the end of mighty Crocodile. You! The Lord of Mud! That's what you've come to.'

She laughed her chuckling, gurgling laugh, and Crocodile writhed with hatred.

But it wasn't hatred that the Witch was after. She tried another way of speaking. 'Think of your eggs,' she said. 'Think of the little ones that called to you as soon as they were hatched. Think of how you carried them one by one to the water's edge, you and Lady Crocodile. No more of that, now. This will be the end of all those little ones.'

Now, Crocodile lay still. From his eyes oozed the tears called Crocodile Tears . . . but they may be real tears for all

we know.

'Help us,' he whispered, in his creaking groan. 'You could help us.'

'Well, yes, I could,' the Witch replied, with a toss of her shoulders that made little rainbows glimmer. 'I am the Witch of Waters, the Queen of Tears, and a powerful singer of songs that move people's hearts ... But then, on the other hand, why should I? You have to tell me. You must make your case. Why should I protect you? Why should I care for you?'

Crocodile was silent. He was getting weaker. His body sank low into the mud.

'Well, after all,' he said, at last, 'I am a murderous and ugly thing. And I am treacherous. Why should you?'

'Yes,' echoed the Witch of Waters, softly. 'You ARE murderous.'

'AND treacherous,' insisted Crocodile. Weak as he was, his eyes still glittered at the thought of his past triumphs, and his cunning. 'Everyone knows the stories of my tricks . . .

I've heard the stories! You see a muddy bank along the riverside, and suddenly, the mud stretches out a claw – that's Crocodile! You see a lumpy roughness in the water, and then, two little glittering, floating eyes – that's Crocodile! You see a drifting log that starts to grin at you with wicked little teeth – that's Crocodile!'

'That's more like it!' cried the Witch, who always loved a story. 'Now that IS Crocodile!'

'That's it,' said Crocodile, proudly. 'That's why you

should save me. Treacherous and ugly as I am, there is no one like me, and I should have my place!'

'Hmmm,' said the Witch. 'Not bad. But after all, you could say the same thing about mosquitos.'

Crocodile was silent, thinking. His wicked eyes sank back into their wrinkly slits.

'Go on,' coaxed the Witch. 'Try again. Remember, it's PEOPLE who are your enemies, right now, and they're such fools, in some ways. They hardly even know what it is they WANT.'

'Well, of course not,' said Crocodile. 'What they really want is too big to imagine. They're really just like the rest of us, underneath. They want Life, which is always a great surprise. They want wildness, though they keep trampling it down with their clumsy ways. They want –'

'Yes,' whispered the Witch of Water, almost holding her breath, for once.

'Mystery,' said Crocodile, at last. 'That's what they want. And what I offer.'

'Ah, Crocodile!' cried the Witch, letting her breath out in a great, long, joyous, rippling sigh, 'that's it! You've got it! Good Crocodile! After all, there is a reason why we two have been friends so long!' In her joy, she gave him a tremendous, watery hug, so that his scales all flashed and glittered with her brightness.

'Thanks, Crocodile! You have said the necessary word! I think you have saved us all!'

Crocodile blinked, suspiciously. 'Saved by a WORD?' he

asked. 'How can that be?'

The Witch of Waters laughed and danced about. 'Oh, Crocodile,' she cried. 'Words are so powerful! They can change hearts. And that's the word that was missing from my song. Now I can sing my song through all the world, and when people hear me, we will all be saved. People will remember what they really love – not more and more Things that clutter up the Earth; not belts and shoes and cases to hold the Things, but MYSTERY – songs and stories and surprises and awesomeness!'

In her excitement, she immediately rushed away, singing the Song of Crocodile, which goes like this:

'O, wondrous and magical ugliness,
O, monstrous Lord of Mud,
Keeper of the wild and secret places –
Help us to preserve the ancient treasure!
Stay with us,
O Guardian of MYSTERY!'

And wherever she went, the roads rolled back and the machines grew silent, and people heard her, and their hearts were changed. They began to love and care for all the wild things in the world – even Crocodile. And Crocodile was saved.

. . . .

Of course, this is only a story. Crocodile is really still in danger, and possibly dying – this part is all too true. But you can make the rest of it come true, too. When you listen to rain and rivers, and the boom and hiss of waves at the edge of the sea, think of Crocodile. Remember the word.

Tell it.

Save the Crocodile

Who's saving the crocodile?

Crocodiles have always been hunted for their skin, which is used to make items like shoes and bags. Because of this there are certain kinds, such as the Nile crocodile, which are seriously endangered. Fortunately there is now a ban on hunting wild crocodiles in many countries, making their chances of survival better.

Still, many need man's help if they are not to disappear completely. There are crocodile farms which breed them for their skins. These farms are a way of stopping crocodiles from dying out, but don't give them a chance to live a normal life in the wild. Far better are the special sanctuaries which have been set up in different parts of the world, where crocodile eggs are hatched and babies are cared for until they are large enough to survive in the wild.

Why save the crocodile?

Crocodiles are odd-looking, fascinating animals, and there's a lot we can learn about nature and the history of our planet by observing them in their natural habitat.

But it's not just important to save them for our own benefit. If crocodiles disappeared it would upset the natural balance of their environment. For example, crocodiles eat certain large fish which in turn prey on small fishes. If there were no crocodiles around, there would be so many of these larger fish that the small fish might soon die out.

Crocodiles and other wildlife are not our possessions. They are really our neighbours on the earth, with as much right to live here as we have. And just as we would help our own neighbours if they were in trouble, we should help the crocodile, now that his way of life is threatened.

QUIZ ANSWERS
1) a,b,d   2) b
3) b   4) b,c,d,e,g

Crocodile's Kin

COLIN McNAUGHTON

Some bestselling Red Fox picture books